The Mystery At Belmont Park

By
Pamela Hillan & Penelope Dyan

Bellissima Publishing, LLC
Jamul, California
www.bellissimapublishing.com

Copyright © 2022 by Bellissima Publishing, LLC

All rights reserved. No part of this book may be reproduced or transmitted in any form or by any means, electronic or mechanical, including any photocopying, or recording, or by any information or storage retrieval system, without permission from the publisher and author.

ISBN 978-1-61477-587-4

First Edition

"Sometimes you just have to step in and do something!"

About The Authors & The Book

Pamela Hillan and Penelope Dyan, lifelong friends who used to like to pretend they were in a Nancy Drew book when they were kids, are back again, all grown up (and then some); and they are still pretending! And this is exactly why the Jan and Jenny books continue to be written and why they began!

Penelope Dyan became a teacher, a published writer, a vocalist, and a mother and an attorney, while Pamela Hillan became a mother and a court reporter . . . and then finally, everything went back to what it was before all of that happened; and the Jan and Jenny books were born, beginning with their very first book in this series, "The Mystery On Burgundy Street".

It was their combined lifelong experiences, and their great desire to do good in this world, along with their love for the law, and their deep concern for others that led to the creation of this latest book in the Jan and Jenny Mystery Series, and to each and every book in this series!

This is the twenty-fourth book in this series; and our heroines, Jan and Jenny (as usual) are out to save the world! This time, they encounter an abused woman and her abuser. And while they initially decide what they are observing is none of their business, they soon discover the problem in front of them is much bigger than they had imagined; and this is why FBI attorney Ms. Wright is called to the scene once again with her team, along with the local police and retired FBI agents Mr. and Mrs. Hufflefinger.

The Mystery At Belmont Park

By
Pamela Hillan & Penelope Dyan

The Mystery At Belmont Park

CHAPTER ONE
A Surprise Call

Much to Jan and Jenny's surprise, Jack and John, the boys from the surf shop near Misty Cove, called Jenny on her cell phone one midday day after school was out for the day, out of the blue, and invited the girls for a day of fun at Belmont Park, a small amusement park fronting Mission Bay Beach. And Jan just happened to be with Jenny at the time, both of them sitting cross legged, Native American style on opposite ends of Jenny's twin bed, laptops open.

"Are you asking us girls out on a date?" Jenny asked, as she put her phone on speaker so Jan could hear everything that was being said.

"It's more like a day with friends," John said from his phone, set on speaker for Jack.

"Will you buy us some cotton candy?" Jenny asked, teasingly.

"Anything you want," John told her. "It happens to be 'boys treat' day," he laughed.

The Mystery At Belmont Park

"Besides," Jack interjected, "it is also pay once and ride all the rides as much as you want!"

"Does that include the fun house?" Jan asked.

"Sure does!" Jack replied.

"And the roller coaster?" Jan added.

"Sure does!" Jack said once again.

"Does that also include corn dogs on a stick, Jack?" Jenny asked, teasing him again, just a bit.

"We can spring for those as well," John interjected. "And we'll even spring for sodas and fries!"

Jan and Jenny looked at each other and smiled.

"Well, what do you think, Jan?" Jenny asked.

"I never turn down a free meal!" Jan laughed.

"There's one more thing," John added.

"And what's that?" Jenny asked.

"You girls have got to promise to not go looking for trouble," John told her in all earnestness.

"Who, us?" Jenny asked.

John sighed.

"Yes, you!" he said. "It seems like every single time we get together with you two girls, we all end up getting into some kind of trouble!"

"Trouble is our middle name!" Jan laughed. "But we never go looking for trouble. Trouble just finds us. That's all. It's not exactly our fault."

"No . . . not exactly . . ." Jack added. "Not exactly," he repeated. "But trouble does seem to find you two!"

"Isn't there something else you need to tell us, or ask us?" Jenny asked, changing the brunt of the conversation.

"Like what?" John asked.

"Like when you propose we're doing this thing, and how we're going to get there," Jenny replied.

"How about we pick you both up at your house, Jenny, at 10:00 AM this coming Saturday? And we will have all day to just have fun!" John said, as Jan looked at Jenny and nodded her head.

"I can spend the night with you, Friday," Jan whispered to Jenny.

To wit, Jenny then told John, "If it's okay with our parents, it's okay with us!"

"Oh . . . and bring your swimsuits and beach towels so we can take a dip in The Plunge," John added as a final thought. "And call us back after you talk to your parents and get the okay."

"Aren't you being a little presumptuous?" Jenny asked. "You're assuming something that is not yet a fact," she added.

"They aren't going to say no to two fine, upstanding lads like ourselves," Jack told her. "Besides, you girls need someone to keep you two out of trouble!"

And as to that, Jan and Jenny had nothing more to say.

And (of course) both sets of parents agreed they could go; and the date (that wasn't really a date) was set in motion,

CHAPTER TWO

THE SLEEPOVER

The weekend was now upon Jan and Jenny; and Jan had packed her backpack for spending the night at Jenny's, not forgetting her swimsuit (and her beach towel) for The Plunge at Belmont Park the following day. (Not to mention that since Jenny's house had a swimming pool, she was never without her swimsuit or a beach towel when she went to Jenny's house.)

Friday nights were the perfect time for good movies and yummy buttered popcorn! Maybe they could even watch a scary movie or two with all the lights out in the house to make it even more frightening! Perhaps they could even watch *three* scary movies!

Jan's mother loved horror movies, so they had quite a collection of very scary DVDs to choose from for movie night. Jan picked three movies that she thought might be appropriate for the occasion and popped them inside her backpack, before it was time to leave for Jenny's house.

Friday night was also bridge night for Jan's parents, so they had made previous arrangements for Cindy, Jan's sister, to stay the night with her Godmother, who lived close by. That left the evening free for Jan to spend the night and the following day with Jenny, and maybe even Sunday too!

"Jan," her father called from across the room, "are you about ready to go? We don't want to be late for our bridge club, and we'll drive you up to Jenny's if you can be quick about it."

Jan shoved her last item into her backpack and quickly zipped it up, running toward the back door to catch her ride.

"I'm ready, dad! Thank you for giving me a lift! That walk up the hill can be tiring."

"No problem, honey," Jan's dad said, as he walked out the back door, joining Jan's mom, who was already seated in the front seat of the car waiting patiently for Jan and her dad.

Once everyone was in the car with seatbelts secured, Jan's dad backed out of the driveway and hurriedly drove Jan to Jenny's house. Upon arriving there, which took only a few minutes, Jan got out of the car with her backpack, and waved goodbye to her parents as they drove off.

Jenny was anxiously waiting for Jan on her front porch. The rest of the family, minus Jenny's dad who was playing his trumpet with the band at the Hotel Del Coronado, were poised for a night of fun!

"Hi, Jan! Did you bring the movies?" Jenny asked excitedly.

Jan smiled, patted her backpack, and replied, "I sure did! I've got three good and scary flicks right in here!"

Then the two girls went into the house, walked straight to Jenny's room, and tossed Jan's backpack on one of the twin beds.

Jan plopped herself down on the twin bed next to her backpack and proceeded to ask Jenny an unexpected question.

"Hey, Jenny, do any of you have some slightly worn clothes in good condition that you don't want anymore?"

"Why? Are you opening a thrift shop or something?" Jenny asked.

"No, silly!" Jan replied. "There's a battered women's shelter in desperate need of articles of clothing of all sizes for the women and children staying there. I heard about it on the radio this afternoon. And I thought it would be a good idea to gather up some things and bring them there."

"I like that idea, Jan! It's a noble gesture worth doing!" Jenny exclaimed. "My mom is always gathering up outgrown clothes and things for the needy! I'm sure we can come up with some nice things to give them. Even my brother, John, has some outgrown things we can add to the donation."

Jan smiled.

"I knew you wouldn't let me down," Jan told Jenny. "That's great!" she added. "Most of these poor women and their kids had to leave their homes so quickly that they couldn't take much with them."

"Why not?" Jenny asked.

Jan shook her head in despair.

"They were afraid of being further mistreated, beaten up (or worse) by their spouses or boyfriends!" Jan replied, looking down at her hands, folded in her lap.

Jenny frowned, concerned.

"It's sad," she said. "And I know there's a lot of that going on these days. We don't know how lucky we really are!"

"That's for sure, Jenny! It's nice to be able to help others any way we can, and this is something we can easily do!" And then, changing the subject, and lightening the moment, Jan suggested they move on to a happier subject! "Let's get to those movies and snacks!" she exclaimed.

And so, the girls made their way to the kitchen, popped some popcorn, and buttered it, grabbed some cold cans of soda, shouted out to everyone in the house that it was time for scary movie night, and headed toward the living room where Jenny's Aunt Vi, her brother John, her mother and her sister, Christine, all joined them.

"I love scary movies!" Jenny's brother, John, said, as he grabbed a handful of buttered popcorn and headed for the kitchen for a soda.

"Bring some sodas for all of us!" Jenny's mother shouted after him.

And for once, Jenny's sister, Christine, said nothing. She was ready to be scared.

Jenny's mom turned off all the lights in the house (without even being asked to do so) and said, "We might as well get in the mood!"

And then everyone laughed, ready to be scared, ready for some fun!

And so, the night began! And what a night it turned out to be! Jan and Jenny even had to pop and butter more popcorn! And Jenny's sister, Christine, fell asleep with her head on Jenny's mother's lap.

CHAPTER THREE
THE NEXT MORNING

Since the boys were picking Jan and Jenny up early, the girls decided they should eat light and save room for the corn dogs, cotton candy, sodas and fries the boys had promised to buy them. And so, they got up, got dressed, went to the kitchen, and ate breakfast bars and vanilla yogurt, downed with a glass of freshly squeezed orange juice.

Jenny quickly, and ever so quietly, ran into her room to pack her backpack, as her Aunt Vi slept with Jenny's sister, Christine, in Christine's room; and Jan grabbed her backpack and the two headed to the living room to wait for the boys to pick them up in the trusty Surf Shop's jeep.

Jenny's dad was still sleeping, but Jenny's mom appeared in her robe to say goodbye to the girls and to peer out the window as they drove away with the boys.

"Have fun on your date?" she said, as the boys pulled up in front of the house and the girls headed for the door.

"It's not a date," Jenny told her mom. "It's friends getting together to have some fun."

"Whatever you say," Jenny's mother said, unconvinced this was simply a day out with friends.

Jenny smiled.

The boys began walking toward the house, as the girls walked out the door.

"My dad sleeps late," she told John, as the foursome headed back to the jeep. "We didn't want you to wake him up by ringing the doorbell," she added by way of explanation.

The boys held the back door of the jeep open for the girls to hop inside.

"Maybe this *is* a date," Jenny whispered to Jan, as the door shut behind them and the boys took their places in the front seat of the jeep (with Jack driving) and as they all buckled up their seatbelts.

"The shocks have been fixed," Jack told the girls, as he started the motor of the open-air jeep and the girls fastened their hair at the napes of their necks with the ponytail holders Jan took out from the zippered front of her backpack. "I know how much you didn't like being bounced around the last time we drove with you girls," Jack added, as he looked back at Jan in the back seat.

"The boy listens," Jan whispered to Jenny.

And then, they were off for a day of fun! And Jenny's mom began to gather lightly worn, used clothes for Jan's project to help the women in the homeless shelter. And for good measure, she also gathered up some old toys for the children that were just gathering dust in the closets.

However, Jenny's sister, Christine, did not like that at all.

"What are you doing?" she asked, as Jenny's mother took a boxed doll from the closet.

"We're gathering things to give to mothers and children who don't have as much as we have," Jenny's mother told Christine. "Jan arranged the whole thing. She told me all about it last night when we were finished watching the scary movies, and after I carried you off to bed."

"But I need that doll!" Christine complained. "I love that doll!"

"But . . . you've never even taken it out of its box!" Jenny's mother protested. "You don't need this," she added, as she continued to gather outgrown toys and clothes from Christine's closet. "And we are all gathering things to help homeless women and children," she added.

Needless to say, Jenny's sister, Christine, was not a happy camper about it; but she acquiesced when Jenny's mother promised to take her on a shopping spree later that afternoon to buy some new clothes and things she thought Christine really needed.

The Mystery At Belmont Park

And meanwhile, the boys parked the jeep in the Belmont Park's parking lot; and the foursome headed for the ticket booth to buy their 'ride everything as many times as you want' amusement park tickets. And then the foursome were fitted with their 'ride all day' wristbands, their tickets to fun!

The Mystery At Belmont Park

CHAPTER FOUR

LET'S GET A LOCKER!

Jan and Jenny, of course, had their trusty backpacks with them that day, loaded with things they thought they might need, including their swimsuits and beach towels. And it just so happened the boys had carefully packed their backpacks as well!

As the four of them walked toward the indoor pool, 'The Plunge', Jan had an idea!

"Hey, guys, since these backpacks are so cumbersome, why don't we get a couple of lockers inside The Plunge building. They have cheap coin lockers in there where we can store stuff like these backpacks (and more) until we need them."

Since the foursome liked the idea, they walked over to the building where the pool was located, and once inside, they picked out two lockers big enough to hold their backpacks, boys' stuff in one locker, girls' stuff in the other. Jack took some change out of his pocket and loaded both locker coin slots.

The girls thanked him.

"I told you two the day was on us!" Jack said, smiling.

John looked around and saw the men's restroom.

"I'm going to go over and use the restroom," he said. "Come with me, Jack," he added, to which Jack agreed. "We'll meet you girls back here when we're finished," he said with a nod.

As they walked away, Jan smirked and shook her head.

"I didn't know boys went to the bathroom in twos, just like us girls," she giggled.

"When you gotta go, you gotta go!" Jenny laughed. And then she added, " It's probably a good idea for us to use the restroom as well before we go on all those wild rides."

"Good idea, Jenny!" Jan quickly replied; and the two of them headed towards the women's restroom, which was just across the hallway from the men's restroom!

And just as the girls started walking toward the restroom, they heard voices arguing.

"That sounds like a domestic dispute, to me, Jenny," Jan whispered. "And the man sounds really angry."

"I think you're right, Jan," Jenny whispered. "Let's get closer and listen."

As the girls walked closer to the arguing couple, they managed to stay around the corner from the couple, well-hidden from sight on the opposite side of the row of lockers.

Jenny, being Jenny, pulled out her phone and started recording the argument.

"In case we need evidence," she whispered.

Jan looked toward the men's restroom and saw Jack and John walking back to where the four of them were supposed to meet. She tugged on Jenny's shirt.

Jenny turned to look at Jan, and suddenly they heard something that sounded like a slap, and then there was the sound of something (which turned out to be someone) being thrown against the steel lockers. It was the woman. And as they peered around the corner of the lockers where they were, they saw her fall to the floor. She was bleeding profusely from her nose.

"Go clean yourself up!" they heard the man say, as the girls quickly retreated again to where they could not be seen.

The woman staggered to her feet, and she went into the women's restroom.

"She should be safe in there," Jenny whispered. "At least she should be safe for the time being," she added. "Do you think we should do something?" Jenny asked.

"I think we should mind our own business," Jan told Jenny stoically.

Then they saw the boys walking in their direction, and Jan and Jenny decided to walk away, as if nothing had happened, and meet up

The Mystery At Belmont Park

with the boys as planned. But neither Jan nor Jenny could hide what they were feeling. They were distraught to say the least.

"I've never seen anything like that," Jan whispered, as they walked toward the boys. "Maybe we've seen worse; but we've never seen anything like that!" Jan added, shaking her head.

"Why does a big burley man like that do that anyway?" Jenny whispered back. "I'll never understand it," she added, as they met up with the boys.

Both boys noticed the girls were upset about something.

"You two look kind of shaken. What's up?" John asked, suspiciously.

"Oh, it's nothing," Jenny said. "At least I hope it's nothing," she added.

"Besides, It's none of our business," Jan interjected.

Satisfied, but somewhat confused by the response, John simply mumbled a feigning acceptance of what he was just told.

"Well, ladies," he finally said, "let's go and have some fun!"

And Jan and Jenny looked at each other, nodded their heads in agreement, and decided at that moment in time that it was truly the best to mind their own business and to have some fun at the amusement park with the boys!

"I can hardly wait to ride the Wild Mouse! And I want some cotton candy too!" Jan excitedly exclaimed, forgetting (for the moment) all about going to the bathroom.

"Don't forget the roller coaster! That's the best ride here!" Jenny added.

John flashed his 'ride all day' wristband (that was fastened securely to his right wrist) in the air, and announced, "Your wish is our command! With these sweet babies on our wrists, we can ride everything in the park as many times as we want!"

It was going to be a great day!

But then, the girls remembered they had some unfinished bathroom business and excused themselves for just a few minutes to take care of their bodily functions before boarding the rides.

CHAPTER FIVE
THE WOMAN IN THE BATHROOM

The girls giggled as they left the boys standing in place and bounded off toward the bathroom. Once inside, they saw the battered woman, still there, attempting to hide her badly bruised and bleeding face with some make-up. The woman saw the girls and suddenly sat down in a heap on the bathroom floor, still holding onto the sink with one hand, her makeup brush still in the other hand.

The woman saw that the girls were distraught.

"I'm fine," she said. "I just had a little accident running into a mirror in the fun house," she told the girls, lying.

"Can we help you?" Jenny asked. "Can we get you anything?"

The woman pointed to her purse sitting on the edge of the sink.

"Could you please hand me my purse?" she asked.

Jan grabbed the woman's purse and handed it to the woman.

"Wow! I suddenly really have to go to the bathroom!" Jenny said, as she headed for the nearest bathroom stall.

"Me too!" Jan said, as she followed suit.

When they came out, the woman was gone, but not before she had taken an unseen swig from the silver flask that was in her purse.

Jan and Jenny washed their hands, dried them, and said nothing as they completed the task, threw away their used paper towels, and headed out the bathroom door.

"I feel really bad for that woman," Jenny finally said.

"Me too," Jan told her, agreeing.

"Do you think she has any children, Jan?" Jenny asked.

"I don't know," Jenny told her. "I mean, she can't be much older than we are."

"She did look terribly young, Jenny. And I really liked the outfit she was wearing . . . all except for the blood on it, that is."

"I sure hope she gets that blood out before it stains that cute outfit," Jenny added.

I think she has more to worry about than some blood on her clothes," Jan told her.

"I wonder if we'll see her around the park," Jenny mused.

"I don't know . . . maybe we will," Jan said.

"I certainly hope she stays safe," Jenny added, but not as an afterthought.

"Now, Jenny, we said we were going to mind our own business; and I am holding us both to that. Today is our day to just have some fun! If the woman needed help, wouldn't she have asked for our help?" Jan asked.

"I don't know, Jan. I just don't know," Jenny said, shaking her head in concern.

"Now, we need to mind our own business and not go looking for trouble, Jenny," Jan said vehemently, as they headed toward the boys again.

And what Jan was saying was completely unlike Jan, but perhaps that was because for once in her young life Jan had no idea about what she could or should do. And neither did Jenny. It was all quite perplexing, to say the least.

The Mystery At Belmont Park

CHAPTER SIX
First Things First

As the girls were walking back to where they'd left the boys, Jenny noticed that the man that was with the battered woman was leaning against a locker. The woman was not with him.

"Jan, look!" Jenny whispered excitedly to Jan, as she clenched Jan's forearm. "It's that horrible man that beat up that woman! He just looks evil to me. Look at his eyes. His eyes remind me of dark, dead pools of water."

"I'll bet he's been an abuser all his life!" Jan whispered back. "I wonder how many other women he's hurt, or maybe even maimed or killed. It looks like he's waiting for her. Do you think he's 'lying in wait' in order to hurt her some more?"

Jenny nodded her head.

"Probably," Jenny replied in a throated whisper, as they continued to walk toward the boys. "I wonder why she puts up with that kind of treatment?"

The Mystery At Belmont Park

"Maybe she thinks it's her fault and that she deserved to be punished," Jan whispered back. "Maybe she doesn't have anyone else to whom she can turn. Or maybe he threatened that he'd kill her if she tried to leave him. I've seen on the news more than once that women are actually murdered by their husbands and lovers in domestic disputes, some disappear, never to be found!"

"That is so sad!" Jenny said, shaking her head in despair, as they approached the boys. "She's probably scared to death. He looks really mean. And he looks really strong! He could really do some major damage to that poor woman. And maybe he already has!"

"Of course, he has!" Jan told Jenny. "But it is still none of our business."

"Where do you think she is now?" Jenny asked, as they approached the boys. "She left the bathroom before we did, and now that guy is standing there alone."

"I have no idea, Jenny," Jan told her.

"Maybe she darted out another exit," Jenny said thoughtfully, as they reached the boys.

"You girls took long enough," Jack teased. "Why do girls spend so much time in the bathroom, anyway? Are you having a party in there or something?" he asked, as the foursome laughed.

"Well, we're here now, Jack," Jenny quipped. "What should we do first?"

The foursome left the building and immediately headed for the Ferris wheel!

"We can ride to the top of the wheel and see everything!" John said, taking charge of the moment. "And there's no line!" he added as they drew nearer.

And so, they went on the ride! Jenny rode with John; and Jan rode with Jack, right behind Jenny and John. Once seated and locked in place by seatbelts, they slowly ascended. It was windy, and the chairs started to rock. Jenny didn't like the rocking motion at all, and frightened, she reached over and grabbed John's arm for security. Her anxiety eased, and John liked the fact that Jenny seemed to feel safer and calmer sitting next to him.

"I'll keep you safe, Jenny," he said. "Just hold on tight!" he added.

Jenny fidgeted and squirmed.

"Doesn't the wind feel great as it gently brushes over your face?" John asked. "Think about how that feels instead of thinking about the rocking motion," John said reassuringly.

And then, they reached the top of the Ferris wheel, and it stopped.

"Why are we stopping?" Jenny shrieked.

"Don't worry, Jenny. They're just letting some riders off and loading new ones," John reassured her.

Jenny felt kind of foolish.

The Mystery At Belmont Park

"Oh. Silly me," she said, still holding tightly onto John's arm.

"The ride's almost over, Jenny, so just relax and enjoy this fabulous view from the top!" John told her. "Just look at that beautiful blue ocean out there! Look at the waves crashing onto the shore! Isn't it spectacular?"

Jenny turned her attention to the view. John was right! It was just beautiful!

Then Jan, who was sitting in the chair with Jack, right behind Jenny and John, yelled out to Jenny, "What a view, huh, Jenny?"

"It's breathtaking!" Jenny yelled back.

And then the Ferris wheel started slowly moving again; and before they knew it, the ride was over; and they all hopped off the ride, ready for a snack!

CHAPTER SEVEN
CORN DOGS AND COTTON CANDY

"Let's have those corn dogs and cotton candy you promised us!" Jan said, as they walked toward the hot dog stand!

"That sounds good to me!" Jack said. "We'll have the corn dogs first, and then the cotton candy!"

"Just like we promised you girls!" John added.

And so, they all got their corn dogs; and they walked through the amusement park eating them, deciding what to do next.

And then, John suddenly stopped in front of the 'guess your weight booth'.

"No way!" the girls screamed in unison, laughing.

"I'm not getting on any scale for anything!" Jenny exclaimed.

"Me neither!" Jan added.

The Mystery At Belmont Park

"It can only lead to eating disorders," Jenny said, as the boys scoffed at them. "I do not want to know what I weigh, and I do not want anyone guessing what I weigh!"

"Me neither!" Jan exclaimed vehemently, as the girls walked away; and the boys scurried off behind them.

"I guess they don't want to be weighed," Jack laughed.

"I guess not," John added.

And the girls hearing them suddenly turned around to confront the boys.

"My body is my business and no one else's!" Jenny said, as a matter of fact.

And then, John spied the cotton candy maker and raced over to grab two cotton candy treats, one for each girl.

Jack followed suit and bought some cotton candy for himself and John, knowing exactly what John was up to now.

"Sweets, for the sweet!" John exclaimed, as he raced back to the girls with the cones of spun pink sugar.

The girls smiled. All was forgotten. And Jack returned with the cotton candy for himself and Jack, and they walked on through the park.

Jan and Jenny had almost forgotten about the young woman in the bathroom when they saw her again. This time she was with the man. They were at one of the carnival-like shooting booths; and he was attempting to now charm the young woman with his prowess.

And, as things would have it, he did win the young woman a prize due to his obvious skills with a rifle. And soon, the woman was carrying a large teddy bear in her arms, all smiles, as she traversed the park.

"I told you it was best to mind our own business this time," Jan told Jenny, as they walked by the shooting booth, and as the woman received her prize, smiling.

"I just don't know. I just don't know," Jenny repeated again. "Something just doesn't feel right."

And then the foursome walked over to the House of Mirrors.

CHAPTER EIGHT

THE ARCADE

Jenny wanted to go into the 'House of Mirrors', but Jan wanted a stuffed animal from the arcade! And as the foursome walked by several different arcade games, on their way to the House of Mirrors, Jan saw a stuffed animal she just had to have!

She grabbed Jack's arm, tugged at it gently, and said in her softest and most persuasive voice, "Jack, would you please play this game of ring toss and see if you could win me that adorable sloth hanging up there?"

Jack smiled.

"Anything for you, pretty lady!" he said, as the foursome walked over to the ring toss and Jack exclaimed, " Give me ten bucks worth of tickets, please!"

Jack took the tickets from the young man running the booth, and he split them up between himself and John, so that Jenny might get a prize won for her, as well; and he started throwing the rings, one by one. Much to everyone's surprise and delight, he was extremely accurate. The girls were impressed!

Jan squealed excitedly.

"Oh, look, Jack!" she exclaimed. "You've won me the sloth! And you still have rings left!"

"I just got lucky!" Jack told her, laughing.

Jan pointed to the stuffed animal (the sloth) that she'd wanted. And the young man took down the sloth and gave it to Jan. (It was almost as big as she was!)

Next, it was John's turn to show off! And that he did! He landed every single ring, winning Jenny whatever she wanted from the highest valued gift table!

Jenny chose a beautiful gold locket (not real gold, of course) but it had beautiful filigree work.

"Maybe we can take some pictures in the photo booth later, and I can put the pictures in the locket," she said. "That way I can remember this day forever," she added, smiling at John.

"Great choice, Jenny!" Jan interjected, as she held the oversized sloth in her arms. "I guess I wasn't thinking too clearly when I wanted this huge sloth. How will it *ever* fit in our locker?"

"I guess you'll just have to drag that thing around with us," Jack laughed, shaking his head. "But it might be a good idea to at least try to stuff it into a locker. It's way too bulky to carry and to take on the rides."

"We might need another locker," John scoffed. "That thing is huge!"

And so, the foursome decided to walk back to The Plunge lockers and to try to stuff the big, bulky sloth into one of the lockers.

But, of course, Jan wanted something to eat first.

"Hey, guys," she said, "I saw a yummy waffle ice cream cone booth a couple of booths back. Let's get some of those first!"

And so, even though they were already filled to the brim with corn dogs and cotton candy, another sweet treat sounded great!

They walked to the ice cream booth, and the boys purchased the cones, and Jack wondered how a little thing like Jan could eat so much!

Jenny looked at Jack, as if reading his mind, and said, "She has a fantastic metabolism!"

And as they downed their ice cream cones on their way back to the locker room, they all laughed; because it certainly seemed like what Jenny had just said was true!

"As for me," Jenny added, as an afterthought, as they walked along, "I'm afraid that I won't be able to eat for days! I just don't have Jan's metabolism!"

You look great to me" John told her . "Whatever you're doing, just keep doing it!"

CHAPTER NINE

BACK TO THE LOCKERS!

Once back at the lockers, Jan (surprisingly) managed to stuff her giant sloth into the locker she shared with Jenny.

"It's a tight squeeze," she said. "But I did it!" she exclaimed.

"Can we please go to the 'House of Mirrors', now?" Jenny asked.

"Only if we can go on the roller coaster after that," John teased.

And then, on the way out of the locker room area, the girls once again saw the young woman who had been beaten. She was leaning on a locker, clutching the teddy bear the man had won for her; and she was crying.

"Keep walking," Jan whispered to Jenny. "Just keep walking. Remember . . . we decided it was none of our business."

Jenny nodded her head, agreeing with Jan.

"I wonder what's wrong with that woman," John mumbled.

"You don't want to know," Jenny told him.

"Sure, I do," John told her. "Maybe we can help her."

The Mystery At Belmont Park

"I thought you didn't want Jan and me to go looking for trouble," Jenny said, as John shook his head.

"And I thought trouble always found you two girls," John replied, with a wry smile.

Jan overheard the conversation.

"It's a domestic issue," she told John. "She's abused. We heard some fighting earlier when Jenny and I were on our way to the ladies' room. We saw her being pushed into a locker; and she fell to the floor, bleeding. And then . . . we saw her in the ladies' room cleaning up when we were in there, and she said she was fine. And not long after that, we saw her at a shooting booth with her abuser, and he won her that big teddy bear; and she seemed okay. And so, then . . . Jenny and I decided (for once) it was none of our business."

"That doesn't sound much like you two girls," John told her.

"We're doing our very best to exercise a modem of self-control," Jenny interjected. "And we're trying to stay out of trouble."

"Well, that will be a first for you two," Jack mumbled, overhearing what was being said.

"Do you think we *should* get involved?" Jan asked Jack.

"I don't know. Maybe," Jack said.

"What is that supposed to mean?" Jan asked.

"It means what it means, and I said what I said," Jack told her. "I think it may be something to be considered," he added. "I had an aunt, my favorite aunt, who was a victim of abuse; and no one would help her, and now she's gone. She's dead. She committed suicide. That's why John and I volunteered at that suicide hotline where the four of us reconnected," Jack told her.

"I'm so sorry, Jack. I didn't know," Jan told him, with tears in her eyes.

And then the foursome decided to return to the locker room to see if they could help the young woman.

"The House of Mirrors can wait," Jenny said.

"And so can the roller coaster," John added.

However, when the foursome got back to the locker room the woman wasn't there. At least she wasn't where Jan and Jenny had last seen her.

CHAPTER TEN

OH WHERE, OH WHERE CAN SHE BE?

As Jan and Jenny, Jack and John, stood by the lockers trying to figure out where the battered woman might have gone, they noticed there was a trail of blood on the floor beginning from where Jan and Jenny had last seen the young woman. So, being in the investigative mood now, they decided to follow the trail.

As they walked, Jenny asked Jan a question.

"Jan, do you (by any chance) have any pamphlets or business cards for that battered women's shelter to which we are donating clothes? If you do, maybe we could find that woman and give her a card or a pamphlet so she can get some help."

Jan thought for a moment.

"That's a great idea, Jenny! And while I don't have anything on me at the moment, I do have some business cards in my backpack

The Mystery At Belmont Park

in our locker! You guys keep following the trail of blood. I'll double back and get her a card out of my backpack in the locker."

Jenny, Jack and John agreed to keep on following the trail of blood as Jan went to get a card for the women's shelter to give to the battered woman.

After a few more minutes of following the trail of blood, John stopped in his tracks.

"Hey, guys," he said, "do you hear that?"

Jack and Jenny stopped to listen.

"Do you hear that whimpering sound that seems to be coming from around the corner?" he asked.

Jack and Jenny nodded their heads in the affirmative, as the three of them headed toward the sound.

There, crouched down in the dark secluded corner, the woman for whom they were searching was crying, with her hands covering her face as if she thought she could simply hide behind her trembling hands.

Jack and John stood motionless, as Jan caught up with the group; and without hesitation, Jan and Jenny walked slowly toward the woman, so as to not frighten or scare her away.

Jenny kneeled next to the woman.

"Excuse me, ma'am, but we couldn't help but hear you crying. Is there anything we can do to help you?" Jenny asked.

The woman removed her hands from her face and looked up at Jenny with tears in her eyes.

"I'm afraid no one can help me," she said, sobbing.

Jan kneeled on the other side of the woman, and gently put her hand on the woman's shoulder, and she held out the card for the woman's shelter with her other hand.

"You're wrong," Jan told the woman. "There's always help available. And there's always hope. All you have to do is call the number on this card. It's a woman's shelter. Someone will come to help you."

The woman shook her head in disagreement.

"You don't understand. He would kill me if he found out I called or went to a shelter. He's a very jealous man. It's either him or me . One of us will end up dead. I know that for a fact."

Jenny looked at Jan in despair.

Then the woman sighed deeply and said, "He was a wonderful man when I first met him. I've tried to leave him several times; but he always pulls me back in, saying he will change and never hurt me again. But actions speak louder than words. I always end up bruised and beaten. He usually stays away from my face, so people don't see the injuries I sustain. But I'm really afraid that he's going to end up killing me someday."

Jan put her arms around the woman as the woman continued to sob.

"You have to be strong," Jan told the woman. " I'm sure this women's shelter could help you as well as protect you."

Suddenly, the woman straightened up and balked in fear.

"No!" she whispered. "You'd better leave! He's coming back. Please, just go!"

Overhearing this, Jack and John rushed over to the girls and grabbed them by their arms.

"Let's get out of here!" Jack said, attempting to pull Jan up from her kneeling position. "I don't want a confrontation with a jealous lover or husband!" he said.

Jack was adamant about them leaving.

It was obvious (at that point) that there was nothing left to do *but* leave. And so, honoring the woman's wishes, the four of them left, with the card tucked tightly in the woman's fist.

And as they hurried off, that (at least) gave Jan a glimmer of hope for the still sobbing woman.

As they walked away they saw the abuser approaching. Averting his gaze and avoiding confrontation, the foursome went back outside to the amusement park rides.

Jan remained very concerned for the woman's safety.

"I sure hope she can get the help she needs before it's too late." Jan sighed.

The Mystery At Belmont Park

"We did all we could, Jan," Jenny reassured her. "We did all we could, at least for the time being," Jenny added. "Let's get our minds off of this for now and go to 'The House Of Mirrors'!"

And so that is what they did. However, 'four gone' (meaning the four of them gone) did not mean forgotten; and Jan (for one) was not ready to lose hope. Because where there was life, there was always hope. And, after all, life was all about hope! At least that was how it was for Jan and Jenny. You see, Jan and Jenny never gave up on anything! And if Jan and Jenny could make something happen, they most assuredly would!

CHAPTER ELEVEN

MIRROR, MIRROR, ON THE WALL!

As the foursome drew closer to the House of Mirrors, Jan began to have second thoughts.

"I'm not sure I want to see myself in a mirror at the moment," she said.

"But why?" Jenny asked.

"I don't want to see how fat I am," Jan told Jenny, to which Jack had an immediate reply.

"You aren't fat," Jack told her. "You're curvy. And I like a curvy girl!" he added, with a grin.

Jan smiled.

"What a nice thing to say," she said.

"I only speak the truth," Jack told her, to which John wholeheartedly agreed.

Jenny was worried about Jan.

"You aren't seeing yourself as you really are," she said. "And that can lead to all sorts of things."

"Like what?" Jan asked.

"For one thing, it could lead to body dysmorphia, Jan. And that's not good. You should never compare yourself to other people."

"Has Jenny been reading an encyclopedia or something?" Jack asked.

"Jenny always has her nose in a book," Jan told Jack by way of explanation.

"Well, Jan," Jenny then said, "please remember that a book is never judged by its cover. It's what is inside of the book that counts! And it's the same thing where people are concerned."

"Do you think that may be why that battered woman doesn't get the help she needs?" Jan asked.

"Maybe," Jenny told her. "I don't know. But I do know that no one should judge anyone by their cover! And beauty comes from inside of a person. And so, don't go thinking negative things about yourself or about how you think you look, because you don't see yourself as others see you."

"I think you're hot!" Jack interjected.

And then, hearing that, Jan decided Jenny was probably right. In fact, maybe that was why the battered woman didn't see herself as she was and why she took so much abuse upon herself.

And Jan finally smiled.

The Mystery At Belmont Park

"Okay! Let's go inside," she said, as the foursome reached the House of Mirrors. "Let's have a heap of fun!" she laughed. "Otherwise, Jenny might keep quoting from the encyclopedia, and I may never hear the end of it!"

And so, the foursome flashed their wristband passes at the ticket taker, and with a nod of his head, they entered the 'House of Mirrors'.

"At least it's not a 'House of Horrors'!" Jan exclaimed, as they walked inside to see what they would see.

CHAPTER TWELVE
IN THE MIRRORS!

As the foursome meandered through the mirrors inside the 'House of Mirrors', they came upon a row of four tall mirrors; and as they each took a stance in front of a different mirror, they started laughing uncontrollably. It was quite a sight to behold!

Jan's mirror made her look very tall and extremely skinny, with an elongated face!

"Now I know what it's like to be tall! I love it!" Jan exclaimed in delight.

Jenny, on the other hand, stepped in front of a mirror that made her look very short and very wide. (She wasn't liking what she saw at all, even though she had always dreamed of being small and petite like Jan was.)

"Well, now I think I'm happy to be me . . . tall in real life!" Jenny laughed. "Just look at me in this mirror! It just isn't me at all!" Jenny added.

The Mystery At Belmont Park

And as they stood where they stood (each standing in front of their own mirror) Jack and John and Jan looked at Jenny's mirror and laughed.

And it appeared that the 'House of Mirrors' was more fun than they had imagined!

In Jack's mirror his body appeared wavy and translucent, like a ghost!

"I'm glad this is just a joke," Jack said. "I'd hate to think I'd ever actually look like this!"

"You might look like that, after you pass on to the other realm," John laughed.

"Don't laugh so hard, laughing boy," Jack teased. "Look in your own mirror, buddy!" he exclaimed with a laugh.

John's mirror portrayed him as a very, very, very tiny man, who was very, very, very roly-poly! And *his* image in the mirror was the most laughable of all! (After all, in real life, John was practically six and a half feet tall!)

After that, because it was so much fun, the foursome took turns looking into each other's mirrors, each standing in front of each of the four mirrors, switching places over and over again, to see what they would look like in each mirror! All in all, they had a great time in that particular mirrored room; but there was even more to see! And so, they proceeded to make their way through the House of Mirrors, forgetting (for the moment) about the battered woman. It was a

The Mystery At Belmont Park

wonderful distraction, especially for Jan who was the most worried about what they had seen and heard when they were last in The Plunge locker room.

The final mirrored room was circular, with way too many mirrors to count; and it was mirrored from floor to ceiling! The mirrors were placed at several different angles, and it caused the foursome to become confused as to whom was really here or there in the large, mirrored room. In fact, it caused Jenny to become quite dizzy. She lost her equilibrium and fell to the floor.

John helped her to her feet.

"I think I've had enough mirrors for today," Jenny said breathlessly, as they exited the mirrored room.

John was concerned and worried about Jenny because of the fall.

"Are you okay, Jenny?" he asked. "I heard a loud thump, and then there you were sprawled out on the floor."

Jenny was embarrassed.

"I'm fine, John," Jenny told John. "I just got a little discombobulated is all."

"Jenny has this cross-dominance, right-left thing, clockwise and counterclockwise issue," Jan interjected. "Sometimes she gets a little bit confused about where she is. It's because both sides of her brain are equally developed, and sometimes the neurons cross and spark or something."

"Now who sounds like a walking encyclopedia," Jenny said, grinning, but not contradicting at all what Jan was saying.

John smiled, as they left the house of mirrors and as they all walked over to a group of palm trees situated by some benches, where the foursome sat down to take a breather before continuing through the amusement park.

As they rested, Jan perused a small map of the area that was attached to a post next to the bench where they sat.

"Hey, guys," she said, "we can ride the Tilt-a-Whirl, the Wild Mouse, and then the roller coaster in no time flat! All we have to do is follow this path in front of us, and we'll hit them in that order!"

Jenny sighed.

"I'm thirsty," Jenny said. "Let's get some snow cones and *then* hit those rides."

And even though Jenny was being a bit presumptuous, the boys *had* promised the girls they could have whatever they wanted; and so, since everyone was thirsty anyway, that is exactly what the foursome did.

"We can have the sodas and fries later," John said, as they headed for the snow cone booth.

The Mystery At Belmont Park

CHAPTER THIRTEEN
THE FROSTY TREATS!

"These rainbow snow cones really hit the spot," Jenny said, as she began to down her snow cone.

The rest of the foursome agreed.

"It certainly takes the edge off a hot day," John said. "But we'll have to finish them before we get on the Tilt-a-Whirl. They don't allow food or beverage on any of the rides."

And so, the foursome found yet another bench on which to sit, so that they could finish their snow cones.

"This reminds me of Hawaii," Jenny said, "except that they call these things shaved ice. But it's basically the same thing."

"Do you know what I like about Hawaii?" Jan asked, without waiting for an answer. "I like the trade winds, the gentle breeze you feel in the afternoon. And the surfing is great!" she added.

"Did you surf the North Shore?" Jack asked.

"You'd better believe it!" Jan told him.

The Mystery At Belmont Park

"When were you in Hawaii?" Jenny asked. "I didn't know you went to Hawaii."

"Oh, we lived there when I was a little kid," Jan told Jenny, as the boys listened. "It was before my sister, Cindy, was born, and right after my dad was stationed in Japan."

"Did you surf the waters of Japan?" Jack asked.

"I was too young," Jan told Jack. "I was basically a baby, a toddler at most."

"It must be fun living in all sorts of different places," Jack said.

"Not really," Jan told him. "I'm just glad to be in one place and to not be moving all the time, now that my dad's put in his twenty plus years and will be retiring soon . . . although, I did like West Virginia," Jan added as an afterthought. "It was so green there!"

"Jan's dad was a commander of a ship," Jenny interjected. "And he's very handsome."

"And Jenny's mother looks like a movie star," Jan added, as the foursome finished their snow cones and threw their paper cones into the nearby trashcan.

"Time for the Tilt-a-Whirl!" Jenny exclaimed. "And don't worry, boys, we will get to that roller coaster!"

And that was that, and Jenny was amazed that she still had some things to learn about her BFF; and Jack was more than intrigued.

And as they reached the Tilt-a-Whirl, they saw the battered woman. She was alone.

"Should we say something?" Jan asked.

"Well, we really can't help her unless she wants to be helped," John told her. "I mean, we can't force ourselves on her."

"Do you think we should report this to someone?" Jenny asked. "Should we call the police?"

"I don't think so," Jack interjected, "not unless we see her being beaten . . ."

Jan shook her head.

"I don't know. I just don't know," she repeated. "If we wait until we see something happen, or until something happens, it might be too late."

And as to that they all agreed. The only questions now were whether they should do something and what it was that they should do if they did something.

And so, they decided to think about it, and they went on the Tilt-a-Whirl. What they didn't know was that the woman's abuser was a chronic, repeat abuser, and that the battered woman they'd encountered was actually a kidnap victim he took with him across several state lines in order to escape arrest and prosecution.

He was also a person of interest in a woman's murder; so, it appeared that the young, battered woman was indeed correct in her assessment of her abuser and had great reason to be afraid. It seemed that in the beginning, she was simply fooled. In looking for love and acceptance, she had fallen victim to a trap.

The Mystery At Belmont Park

But exactly who was this woman? That was the mystery yet to be solved. And if anyone could solve the mystery of whom this woman was, and of whom her abuser actually was, it would most assuredly be Jan and Jenny.

And so, they rode the Tilt-a-Whirl and when they got off the ride, the battered woman (who was alone) standing by the ride when they got on the Tilt-a Whirl was gone.

"I wonder where she went?" Jan asked, not expecting an answer, because of course, the others had no way of knowing that.

And, still spinning from the effects of the ride, the foursome moved on, all deciding to keep their eyes open for the battered woman and her abuser.

So, according to plan, they went on to ride the Wild Mouse, all the while keeping their eyes open, looking for the battered woman, hopefully minus her abuser to avoid any confrontation with him. (And of course, they had no idea how dangerous her abuser actually was.)

As they left the Wild Mouse, and as Jan and Jenny smoothed their now windblown hair, Jenny said, "Wow! That was fun! Why don't we head for the roller coaster next?"

And so, all agreeing, off they went to the roller coaster.

CHAPTER FOURTEEN
THE GIANT DIPPER

The day went on, and Belmont Park became packed with visitors. Jan and Jenny were not big fans of waiting in long lines, and Jan and Jenny hoped the roller coaster, commonly referred to as 'The Giant Dipper', wouldn't have them waiting in a long line.

Unfortunately, there were several people already in line when they arrived at the ride, and Jan noticed one couple in particular.

Jan nudged Jenny as they walked to the back of the line.

"You'll never guess who's going to be in front of us on this ride," she whispered to Jenny.

It was the battered woman and the abuser.

As the foursome got in line behind the battered woman and her abuser, they looked at one another, astounded, but said nothing.

Jan and Jenny got in line behind the boys so as to not startle the woman, thinking that maybe she wouldn't notice them; but she did. Nevertheless, the battered woman kept her cool, remained calm, said nothing to the girls, and showed no obvious glimmer of recognition whatsoever.

"This ought to be interesting," Jan whispered to Jenny. "You and I can take the two seats in the front of the car, right behind them, and Jack and John can then sit behind us. We need to be observant!"

As the amusement park became more and more crowded, the temperature was increasing in more than one way for Jan and Jenny.

"I sure hope this line moves fast," Jenny told Jan. "I'm getting really hot just standing here."

"That's because you *are* hot!" John mused, as he grinned at Jenny. "Don't worry too much about the wait," he added. "They seat about sixteen people at a time when the cars come in, since each car is attached to the one in front of it; and all the cars (since they are attached to each other) will go up at once. I'm sure the wait won't be too long at that pace."

Hearing what John had just said did little to ease Jenny's building anxiety. And Jack and John hadn't even noticed that the battered woman and her abuser were now standing in line in front of them.

Finally, the line began to move, and people were both leaving the roller coaster ride and being seated on it somewhat simultaneously. As it turned out, the battered woman and her abuser were seated in the third to last car in the line of cars in the back of the double-benched car seats, behind an elderly couple who were out for

The Mystery At Belmont Park

a day of fun. The foursome piled into the next car, Jan and Jenny in the front seats, Jack and John sitting behind them. As the seats were taken everyone fastened their seatbelts and waited to roll on the tracks to the very top of The Giant Dipper, before it made its exciting first, long drop down.

As the line of cars began ascending to the top of the tracks, the battered woman and her abuser began to argue. And the argument became more and more intense as the cars rose higher and higher on the tracks.

The passengers on the ride were screaming in delight even before they reached the pinnacle of the ride. Jan pulled Jenny over to whisper into Jenny's ear as she saw the woman's abuser reach over and unfasten the abused woman's seatbelt.

"It looks like he's trying to throw her out of the car!" Jan exclaimed aloud now, knowing that with all of the screams, she wouldn't be heard by anyone else except Jenny.

Jenny looked at the battered woman. She was struggling and yelling at the man and pushing him away, trying to defend herself.

The car in which the foursome were sitting neared the top of the ride, seventy-five feet into the air. The view at the top was spectacular! And even though it lasted only a few seconds, it was, indeed, a beautiful view of the ocean and the beach below it. And then . . . down they dropped, speeding along the curves and the ups and downs of the track, with everyone screaming with excitement. Jan was so exhilarated she started to laugh uncontrollably. Jenny gasped for breath. (All in all, it was very exciting!) Down and around, they went, and then up high again they went. It was hard to concentrate on the battered woman and her abuser now while they were having so much fun on the ride. However, Jan and Jenny knew they had to focus on the couple, no matter how difficult that was! After all, they could *always* take *another* ride on the roller coaster.

And then . . . Jan and Jenny noticed something as the roller coaster came to a stop. The battered woman was no longer sitting in the back of the roller coaster car in front of them, and there were sirens, and a lot of flashing lights.

And the man who was with the battered woman was suddenly gone as well. He had managed to slip away in all of the excitement of the moment. But where had he gone? And where was the battered woman? Jan and Jenny looked at the boys, who were just as bewildered as they were.

And then . . . Jenny saw Ms. Wright, the attorney from the FBI; and Jan saw Ms. Wright as well. And soon the truth would be revealed.

CHAPTER FIFTEEN

BUT WHY ARE YOU HERE?

The foursome scurried over to where Ms. Wright was standing, and she motioned to the police authorities that it was okay for them to enter the cordoned off space around what appeared to be a crime scene. The girls immediately ran to Ms. Wright's side; and she hugged the girls, and she welcomed Jack and John with handshakes.

"It's good to see you boys again," Ms. Wright said, as she shook their hands, one at a time, remembering their last encounter rounding up the fentanyl culprits.

"It's good to see you too!" Jack said, wondering why she was there.

"But why are you here?" Jan asked, as she saw Mr. and Mrs. Hufflefinger in the distance, walking up toward where they stood.

"Well," Ms. Wright began, "I thought I would take a little vacation, a breather of sorts, here in San Diego; and I was visiting with my old friends, the Hufflefingers, when I received a text and video from Jenny. Of course, the Hufflefingers, being retired FBI agents (Ms. Wright explained for the benefit of the boys) were able to trace the origin of the call; and when I ran the faces in the video through CODA, I came up with identity hits right away."

Jan looked at Jenny in disbelief.

"I forgot to tell you, with everything else going on," Jenny told Jan, "that when I was taping the woman and her abuser (when we first saw them on the way to the bathroom earlier) that I was doing a video. And I sent the video to Ms. Wright . . . just in case."

"Just in case?" Jan asked, surprised that Jenny had not told her earlier that she had contacted Ms. Wright.

"Well," Jenny began, "I really didn't think there was anything there; but I had this feeling about it."

"Do you mean the knowing thing?" Jan asked.

"I guess so," Jenny told her. "But I just thought maybe I was overreacting."

"Well, you weren't overreacting," Ms. Wright told Jenny, as they saw the battered woman being loaded onto a stretcher and being put into an ambulance.

"Is she alright?" Jan asked.

"Fortunately for her," Ms. Wright told the foursome, "a supply cart loosely piled with flour and powdered sugar was happening by on its way to the donut trailer, and the driver paused to readjust its contents, just as the woman was falling. She landed right on top of it all, and it tempered her fall."

"What does that mean?" Jack asked, as John said nothing.

"It means she broke some bones; but that she will ultimately survive," Ms. Wright told John, as she took a pause before continuing. "But . . . she did say something before she lost consciousness," Ms. Wright added.

"She did?" Jenny asked in surprise.

"Well, actually . . . she said two things. She said two girls who tried to help her saw the whole thing, and I am thinking that just might be you and Jan," Ms. Wright told Jenny.

"Well, we didn't see the whole thing," Jan interjected. "But we did see the man unfasten her seatbelt, and we can say he was abusing her all day."

"And what is the second thing she said?" Jenny asked, ever quizzical.

"She said she stabbed him in the side with her metal nail file, as he pushed her out of the roller coaster car, and that she wanted the two girls who tried to help her to know that she stood up for herself. And then, right after that, she lost consciousness."

"If she stabbed him," Jan said, "maybe there's a blood trail that will lead us to him!"

And by that time, Mr. and Mrs. Hufflefinger were inside the police boundary lines with Ms. Wright and the foursome.

"Now, you girls be careful!" Mrs. Hufflefinger told the girls, as she beamed with pride.

And then . . . off the foursome went . . . in search of yet another bloody trail!

And Ms. Wright directed two men on her FBI team to follow the foursome, but to keep their distance until needed.

Jan and Jenny, and Jack and John, had yet to learn the truth behind the mystery of the young, battered woman. They still did not know she was a kidnap victim or how young she was when she was taken across state lines, and that the battered young woman's kidnapper was a serial abuser of special interest in the murder of yet another young woman. All they knew (for now) was that they were in search of a bloody trail.

CHAPTER SIXTEEN
IN PURSUIT

What had started out as a fun day of food and amusement park rides for the teen foursome, now turned into a search for a violent criminal.

Jan and Jenny, of course, took it all in stride; because things (not unlike what was happening right now) just seemed to happen to them. However, Jack and John weren't quite as used to it, even though they had been through two previous sleuthing encounters with the girls. However, they were brave souls; and they felt obligated to protect the girls as they pursued the criminal at hand. So, with no reluctance at all, they tagged right along with the girls on their quest.

Jenny was trying to figure out how this man was able to slip by them so easily, as well as how he managed to push the abused woman out of her seat on the roller coaster without anyone noticing it. She decided that with all of the screaming and excitement on the ride, everyone on the ride was distracted (including herself and Jan) and that it just happened. But that didn't quite explain why those on the ground hadn't seen anything. Jenny recalled there were several times during the ride when their heads were being thrown forward and back with all the deep drops and sharp turns during the ride; and she decided that this in combination with all of the excitement, more than likely interfered with the observational abilities of herself and Jan, even though they had been determined to focus on the battered woman and her abuser.

"Yes!" Jenny thought to herself. "It is entirely possible we were merely distracted!"

However, now it was time to backtrack and to try to find the starting point of this man's departure from the ride.

As Jan and Jenny, and Jack and John, walked back to the roller coaster, Jan offered her opinion on the manner of the abuser's escape.

"I've been thinking," she began, "since we didn't really see the man when the roller coaster finally stopped that maybe when we came to that really slow speed at the very end of the ride, he may have jumped out. If there is a blood trail from her stabbing him, I think that's where we should look first."

Jenny thought for a moment.

"If she stabbed him in his side (like we were told) she may have hit the abdominal aorta," Jenny explained. "The abdominal aorta supplies blood to the lower portions of the body, including the legs; and it is one of the major arteries of the human body."

Jan shook her head.

"I told you she's a walking encyclopedia!" Jan quipped.

"And in this case that is probably a good thing, because it means we might be able to find a substantial blood trail!" Jack exclaimed, as John flashed a smile in Jenny's direction.

Since the ride had temporarily been shut down due to the accident and the investigation of an attempted murder, there was complete access to the roller coaster ride, compliments of Ms. Wright and the authorities. And so, the foursome were allowed access to the underpinnings of the rollercoaster.

Jenny took out her cell phone and turned on the flashlight option. The rest of the foursome followed her lead and did the same.

Lights lit, the foursome began their explore underneath the old wooden roller coaster.

"Now, keep a good eye out, guys," Jan said. "Blood is dark and difficult to see. If we get lucky, we'll find some kind of clue or evidence that he was here," Jan added, almost as if she was in charge of the pursuit.

The search began. Jack and John took one side of the roller coaster's track, Jan and Jenny took the other side of the roller coaster's track.

Then Jenny noticed something.

"Look, Jan!" she shouted. "There's some kind of a service door under here! Maybe it leads to the outside of the park. I'll bet this is how he escaped."

And then she saw the blood on the ground leading right up to what appeared to be some sort of a service door.

Jan ran to the door, with Jenny close behind her; and she grabbed the doorknob. It was wet . When she looked down at her hand and focused the light from her cell phone (that she held in her other hand) on her now wet hand, she saw that the wet substance was blood. She wiped the blood on her shorts, remaining calm and composed.

"I think you're right, Jenny," she said, as the boys stood quietly by the girls, and the two FBI agents remained distanced from them, observing everything that was happening. "He went through this door, and he probably jumped from his seat when we slowed down coming into the end of the roller coaster ride. We've apparently found his trail. Let's see where it leads."

And then Jan opened the door.

CHAPTER SEVENTEEN
BEHIND THE DOOR!

As the door opened, and as the girls peered inside of what appeared to be a service room and the heart of the mechanics that ran the roller coaster, they didn't know what to think. Was there yet another door to the outside, or was the battered woman's abuser still inside of this room?

Jenny trembled as the foursome entered the good-sized room.

"I don't see a way out of here," Jenny said.

It was dark inside the room, and Jack and John looked around for a light switch. Since they were the last of the foursome to enter the room, they'd left the door open out of a sense of precaution, since they had seen the two FBI agents following them and felt it wouldn't be out of line to assume they just might need some assistance.

Jan and Jenny had no idea they were being trailed. The girls told the boys to remain guard at the door . . . just in case.

The Mystery At Belmont Park

John found the light switch, and he turned on the lights.

"That's much better," he said, as the old fluorescent lights overhead flickered.

Jan and Jenny left the boys guarding the door and began their search behind the several rows of electronic equipment racks to see what they could find, if anything,

There was no door leading to the outside. So, was the battered woman's abuser still here? Or was he ever here at all? Was this merely a well set up ruse by a clever criminal?

Not long after that, the two FBI agents entered the room, unseen by Jan and Jenny, who were searching amidst the floor to nearly ceiling-high racks of electronic equipment that ran the roller coaster . . . but who were happily welcomed by Jack and John.

And finally, as the girls reached the last of the racks, they saw a doored workbench with a barstool sized chair strewn to the side.

I'll bet he's inside of there," Jenny said, pointing to the workbench doors.

"There's no way out," Jenny whispered.

"Do you think he's armed?" Jan asked.

"Who knows?" Jenny told her. "But I think it's best to not take any chances," she added, as Jan agreed; and the boys with the two FBI agents finally came upon them.

The girls recognized the men as part of Ms. Wright's FBI team, but there was more.

The Mystery At Belmont Park

There was a pool of blood seeping out from under the closed doored workbench, and there was a lot of blood, unnoticed by the girls until now; and it appeared obvious the battered woman's abuser was hiding behind those doors.

Was the culprit dead or alive?

Jenny trembled, but Jan was confident. The boys had no idea what they should think. And the two FBI agents walked over to the workbench.

The answer to the question of whether the abused woman's abuser was hiding behind those workbench doors was now before them and was soon to be answered.

CHAPTER EIGHTEEN
THE BEGINNING OF THE END

"Do you think he's dead?" Jan whispered to Jenny, as the two FBI agents drew closer to the doors beneath the workbench.

"That's hard to say," Jenny whispered back to Jan, and the two boys listened intently. "You see, the abdominal aorta is fixed in the back of the abdominal cavity just to the left of the lower thoracic and lumbar spine. It spans from the left gastric artery to the bifurcation into the iliac arteries. People who have been stabbed, like we think this guy was stabbed, have had cuts to their abdominal aorta and have survived. And it seems to me that even the longest of steel nail files could only nick that artery at best, if at all, although it is possible since our culprit is quite lean and thin with little muscle. If he is still alive, he might yet be saved," Jenny added.

"I think that's more information than I wanted to know," Jan whispered.

The Mystery At Belmont Park

"How do you know all of that?" Jack asked, ever so quietly.

"I just read it to you off my cell phone," Jenny told him. "I just now googled it. I couldn't stand the suspense of wondering."

"Well," Jan smirked, "I didn't think you had an encyclopedia with you . . ."

Jenny took a deep breath and then sighed.

"Get back! Get way back!" one of the FBI agents demanded, as he drew nearer to the doors beneath the workbench. "We do not know if this guy's armed!"

The foursome stepped as far back as they could possibly go, and they leaned against the last of the electronic equipment racks.

"It's probably better if you just leave and wait outside!" the other FBI agent directed.

"Sounds good to me, girls," John said. "Let's get out of here!"

"Oh, darn," Jan mumbled, as they headed to the door to leave the room. "Now we won't get to see how this all turns out!"

"That's fine by me," Jenny told her.

"Better safe than sorry," Jack added.

And then, before they knew it, the foursome were outside the room.

"Now what?" Jenny asked.

"Now we wait and see," Jan told her.

And then they heard a single gunshot.

"I wonder what just happened," Jenny said, trembling.

"Whatever happened in there, we've probably seen worse," Jan confessed.

The boys said nothing at first, and then Jack spoke.

"We should just be happy we're out here and safe," he said. "That bullet could have been meant for one of us. And besides, those FBI guys know exactly what they are doing."

"I suppose so," Jan told Jack, very unconvincingly.

"I'm just glad we are where we are," Jenny said, as John nodded his head.

"It's best that we're out here," John added, confirming Jenny's statement.

And then the foursome just stood there outside the now closed door and waited.

Inside, the abuser brandished a gun. He'd gotten off one random shot that wasn't intended to actually kill anyone. It was more of a statement.

"Go ahead and shoot me!" he demanded. "I'm not worth saving!"

"Maybe we should just leave you inside that box to bleed to death," one of the two FBI agents said.

"I don't think that's what he really wants," the second FBI agent told the first. "Otherwise, he wouldn't have torn his shirt and have tried to stop the bleeding by stuffing that piece of his shirt into his open wound."

The Mystery At Belmont Park

"I'd rather die now, than be faced with what I'm about to face," the man said, gasping for air.

"I'm afraid that's not your choice," the second FBI agent said. "We aren't going to let you commit suicide by provoking us to shoot you. You need to be tried and punished for your crimes."

"What crimes?" the abuser asked defiantly, as he held the gun in his hand to his head.

And then, before a shot could be fired, the first FBI agent lunged at the man, and because the man was in a weakened state, he was unable to resist.

The gun fell from his hand, and the second FBI agent picked it up and bagged it for evidence.

And then an ambulance was called, and before anyone knew it, two paramedics with a stretcher rushed through the door where the foursome stood just outside of the room; and the man was whisked away in a waiting ambulance.

It was starting to get late.

Once the paramedics had removed the bleeding man, the two FBI agents exited the room, after cordoning off the area for the gathering of any trace evidence or any other evidence. The roller coaster remained closed, and it would remain closed until all the evidence surrounding the matter at hand could be retrieved.

The Mystery At Belmont Park

"I guess we won't be riding the roller coaster again today," Jenny said, after they were debriefed briefly by the two FBI agents and were then directed to leave the immediate area.

"I guess we can always ride the Ferris wheel!" Jan quipped. "Or maybe we should go to The House of Horrors," she added.

"I think we've seen enough horror for today," Jenny told Jan, to which the boys nodded their heads in agreement.

But the day was not over, and there was more to be said and done. And that is why, as the foursome left the roller coaster, trying to decide what they should do next, they were met by Ms. Wright and the Hufflefingers.

And soon they would know everything.

The Mystery At Belmont Park

CHAPTER NINETEEN
Lunch On The Boardwalk

Meeting up with Ms. Wright and the Hufflefingers was the perfect ending for a day that had turned out to be so stressful. The girls got great comfort from the three of them, and whenever either Ms. Wright or the Hufflefingers showed up, the girls felt safe; and that was really saying something for our two brave sleuths, especially for ever-anxious Jenny.

Ms. Wright invited everyone to a late afternoon lunch at a fancy restaurant on the Mission Beach boardwalk, that had a view of the beautiful, expansive Pacific Ocean! It was within walking distance from Belmont Amusement Park, so they didn't have to worry about driving anywhere.

"I've been told this restaurant has some of the best seafood entrees in San Diego," Ms. Wright said, as they all walked toward the restaurant. "And . . . I strongly suggest that we all take advantage of that! The tab is on the FBI; so, enjoy!"

Jenny loved seafood, and so did Jan.

"I can hardly wait to get that menu in my two hands," Jan told Ms. Wright.

"I wonder what the Catch of the Day is," Jenny mused.

Jack and John weren't at all excited about eating fish after all of the junk food they'd eaten earlier in the day; but they were troopers, and they did want to please the girls. And they were boys, after all, so they always seemed to find room for food!

"At least we won't be picking up the tab on this one," Jack told John as they followed behind the others.

Mrs. Hufflefinger overheard the comment and smiled.

"It certainly is good to see you girls again," Mrs. Hufflefinger said, as they all walked up to the restaurant.

Arriving at the restaurant was an experience in itself. It was a three-story, ultra-modern, all glass enclosure, resembling something a person might expect to see in outer space, a magnificent work of architecture that really intrigued John, especially since he wanted to be an architect someday.

Inside, there was a long, winding spiral staircase leading up to the third-floor restaurant seating. Huge aquariums filled with the most beautiful saltwater fish casually swam about in sea-like grottos built inside huge floor to ceiling aquarium tanks.

The Mystery At Belmont Park

"Wow!" Jan exclaimed, "I've never seen aquariums like this! I can't even imagine how hard it is to keep them clean! I used to have a small aquarium, and it was a lot of work!"

Jack laughed.

"Yep. I know all about that!" he said. "My parents have a pretty big aquarium at home; and you're absolutely right, Jan. It is a lot of work!"

Once they reached the top of the long, winding spiral staircase, the party of seven was seated. And . . . as providence would have it, they were seated right next to the expansive floor to ceiling windows that overlooked the glorious ocean! And Jan and Jenny felt as though they could reach out and touch the ocean waves as they crashed against the shoreline down below them.

Jenny was in love with the whole vibe. She loved the ocean and everything about it!

"This is so beautiful! I hope someday I can have a home by the ocean," Jenny sighed, as she looked out the windows at the view below her; and then she perused the menu.

"I'm delighted that you approve of my choice," Ms. Wright told her. "Now, let's order some food!" she added. "I'm famished!"

Orders were placed and served; and they all had a great time as they ate heartily, doing their very best to keep the main subject now at hand in the background, at least for now.

However, Jenny, being Jenny, could not help being anxious.

The Mystery At Belmont Park

And then, just as they were finishing their desserts, Ms. Wright's phone rang.

CHAPTER TWENTY
BACK TO REALITY

Ms. Wright listened as the caller related the news. She had a scowl on her face. Jan and Jenny couldn't help wondering what the caller was saying, but they knew better than to ask Ms. Wright about that. So much was confidential with the FBI, especially with matters such as these. After all, it was always best to not say or do anything that could interfere in any way with any sort of future prosecutions that may or may not occur.

But this wasn't exactly one of those conversations. It was what one might call a 'mixed bag' conversation. There was some good news, and also maybe some bad news, depending on how you looked at it . . . hence, the scowl on Ms. Wright's face as she listened attentively to the caller and finished the call.

"I see," Ms. Wright told the caller. "Thanks for keeping me updated."

The Mystery At Belmont Park

The waitress filled Ms. Wright's coffee cup.

"I shouldn't drink so much coffee," she said, as the waitress left. "But the caffeine keeps me going on days like this," she added.

The others at the table said nothing, but the Hufflefingers, both being retired FBI agents, knew something was wrong, or just maybe that something was right.

The boys, unlike Jan and Jenny (and having little experience in these matters) were somewhat ambivalent over the whole thing, while Jan and Jenny knew something was definitely afloat.

Ms. Wright slowly sipped on her coffee, as Mrs. Hufflefinger straightened the white cloth napkin on her lap and said, "I hope it wasn't bad news, dear."

The waitress returned and filled the Hufflefingers' coffee cups.

"I don't know," Ms. Wright told her. "I'm trying to absorb it all."

"Is the woman all right?" Jan boldly asked.

"Oh, yes. She's fine. In fact, she's talking about you girls and wants to see you two," Ms. Wright told Jan. "It's just that things have just gotten a bit complicated."

"Things always get complicated in matters such as these," Mrs. Hufflefinger said.

"We're here to help you in any way we can," Mr. Hufflefinger added.

The Mystery At Belmont Park

The boys said nothing, as the waitress came by again with free refills on the foursome's sodas.

"Ice cold soda sure hits the spot on a hot day like this," Jenny said, attempting to moderate the feeling of tension in the air.

Ms. Wright knew what Jenny was trying to do; and so, she decided to just tell them all about the call. After all, it would all more than likely hit the media outlets and become common knowledge not before too very long.

"I'm going to debrief you all," Ms. Wright finally said.

And so, on bated breath, they all waited for the big reveal.

CHAPTER TWENTY-ONE
EVERYONE HAS A STORY

Meanwhile . . . the abuser was now lying on a hospital bed in the hospital under the careful protection and watch of the FBI, with a guard on him at all times.

As he lay there, he began speaking to the agent on guard.

"I don't care what y'all do to me now," he said." It can't be any worse than what I've had to endure. You see, my mother left my father, because he abused her; and she went from one abusive man to another, never seeming to break the pattern of abuse. And she took it all out on me! She dragged me around from one place to another for all of my childhood. That's how we survived . . . my mother went from one man to the next."

The agent listened attentively, as the abuser continued, even though the battered woman's abuser was weak from the loss of blood and probably should have saved his energy.

"I never really knew my father," he said, as he drifted in and out of consciousness. "And the men she partnered with after that, were just like him; and they often beat me, and so did she, even for the smallest of offences. In fact, I pretty much got slapped around all the time. I have scars where I was burned with cigarettes. As I grew older, she became an alcoholic; and no one wanted her as her good looks faded, and her skin yellowed from liver disease. That's when I learned to fend for myself. I dumpster dived for food. Sometimes the people in restaurants would leave me food out in the back of their establishments. When I was twelve my mother died of cirrhosis of the liver."

"Everyone has a story," the FBI agent interrupted. "Even I have a story. Life is about the choices you make."

"Well, after that, I became a foster kid. I was put into the system. No one ever really wanted me, not ever. And in the system, I was nothing more than a paycheck for those who took me into their homes. And if I stayed a year anywhere, that was nothing more than a small miracle."

"Like I said," the FBI agent repeated, "everyone has a story. Even I have a story. Albeit, your story is sadder than most."

Fighting to stay conscious and awake in fear of death, the abuser continued.

"I aged out of the system at eighteen, and I turned to the streets. I committed small crimes. I broke into cars and into the homes of people when they weren't there. I'd watch their houses until they left. Then I'd go inside and rob them. That's how I survived until I managed to get a job at a gas station. I was lonely. And since I'm a decent looking man, I didn't have any trouble meeting women; but I took my past out on the women I was with."

"That's called patterning," the FBI agent interjected. "But patterns can be broken."

"I hated my mother for what she did to me. In my mind, no matter how hard I tried to not feel the way I was feeling, all women were trash and didn't deserve to live. And I learned to manipulate them. And I even killed one of them, and maybe I even killed two of them," the battered woman's abuser said, as he lay there thinking about what happened on the roller coaster. And then he added, "If I saw a woman I wanted, and she didn't want me, I just took her, and I locked her up; and then she was mine until I tired of her."

"That's called kidnapping and murder," the FBI agent said, as the battered woman's evil abuser began to helplessly gasp for breaths between his words.

"It don't matter anymore what you do to me," he said. "I've seen the worst of mankind; and I've become the worst kind of man," he added, as he lost consciousness, and his breathing stopped.

The doctors rushed in as the monitoring alarms sounded, and they tried to revive him. They even tried the paddles. But it was of no use now. He was dead. He was gone from this earth forever. It was indeed a sad way to break the pattern of abuse he had wrought upon others.

CHAPTER TWENTY-TWO
THE DEBRIEFING

Ms. Wright looked around the table, wide-eyed, and finally fixed her eyes on Jan and Jenny.

"The abuser is no longer with us," she said.

"You mean he escaped?" Jan asked.

"No, I mean he is dead," Ms. Wright said.

"Is that the good news or the bad news?" Jan precociously asked.

"Like I said, it's a mixed bag. It's sad when anyone dies. We always hope, and we like to think, that even the worst among us have some glimmer of good in them and can be rehabilitated."

Jan fumbled with the cloth napkin on her lap.

"I haven't thought about it that way," she said, lowering her eyes.

"And what is the good news?" Jenny asked.

The Mystery At Belmont Park

"Besides the fact that I don't have to take this to trial, we found the battered woman's parents; and they are flying in tonight, and they will take her home with them as soon as she is able to travel," Ms. Wright added.

Jenny was relieved.

"But there's a hitch," Ms. Wright told them. "There will be a coroner's inquiry into the death of her abuser. So, you four will have to testify under oath and provide statements as to exactly what you saw and heard from beginning to end."

"That sounds reasonable," Jenny said.

"But why?" John asked, as Jack remained silent and the Hufflefingers said nothing.

"We need to show this was a justifiable homicide," Ms. Wright explained. "And while there is no doubt as to that in my mind, testimony will have to be provided."

"Is that all?" Jack asked, finally speaking. "We all saw and heard just about everything, and he did push her from the roller coaster."

"Jan and I saw him unfasten her seatbelt," Jenny said. "And then the next thing we knew, she was gone."

"The question will be whether she stabbed him first, initiating the assault," Ms. Wright told the foursome. "And this is why we need you four to establish the abuse you observed."

The girls looked at each other, bewildered.

"Hasn't she been through enough? Jan asked, with tears welling in her eyes, but not expecting a response.

"Well, the good news is we have a dying declaration of sorts from the abuser. And we know the woman is a kidnap victim. She was taken from out front of a Walmart Store in Nevada two years ago. She was only sixteen years old, below the legal age of consent."

"But she said he was kind to her at first," Jan told Ms. Wright. "I don't understand."

"When someone is kidnapped like she was, and then becomes dependent on their kidnapper for the basic necessities of life, they become confused, not believing anything can ever get better; and then they grow strangely attached to their captor. It's called Stockholm Syndrome, and sometimes they will do anything to please their abductor."

"But I think she was just afraid to leave," Jan interjected, shaking her head in dismay.

"It's a very sad state of affairs," Ms. Wright then said. "And it appears that he did murder a woman before he kidnapped this woman. Facial recognition matches and a DNA match to DNA taken from the murder scene will prove he committed the earlier murder beyond a reasonable doubt, even though it doesn't really matter now, except for giving the murdered woman's family closure."

"What else, besides testifying at the coroner's inquest can we do to help? Jenny asked.

The Mystery At Belmont Park

"Just be a friend to the woman and let her know you care," Ms. Wright told them. "She will have a lot of healing to do now, both mentally and physically. She will need to learn to trust others again. And since she asked for you two in particular," Ms. Wright added, with a nod of her head at the two girls, "it appears she does trust you to some extent already; so, you have a head start on that."

"That's easy!" the girls said in unison.

"We can do that!" Jan added.

"And Mr. Hufflefinger and I will do anything and everything we can," Mrs. Hufflefinger said.

And so that is exactly what they all did, with a little help and support from Jack and John and Mr. Hufflefinger, that is.

And after a time of healing and love, the kidnapped, abused young woman was able to return home. She was not charged in the death of her abuser, as his death was conclusively concluded to have occurred in self-defense. And as for the future ahead of her? A new life story was now only beginning. And it was, indeed, a story filled with love.

"And what will your life story be? Only time will tell. And time never tells its secrets, as we well all know."